Smriti Prasadam-Halls   illustrated by Alison Brown

I Love You Night and Day

BLOOMSBURY

NEW YORK   LONDON   NEW DELHI   SYDNEY

I love you most, I love you best,
Much, much more than all the rest.

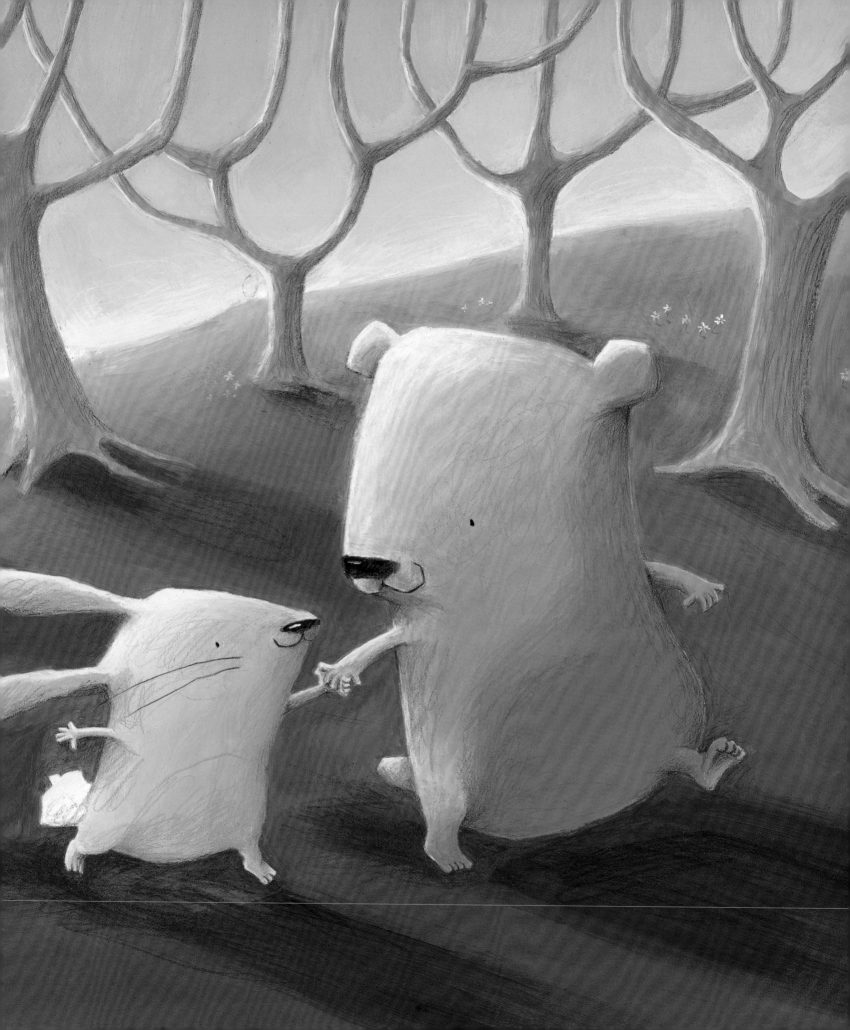

I love you tall, I love you high,

Way up in the sunny sky.

I love you far, I love you wide,

From over here . . .

. . . to the other side.

I love you low, I love you deep,
Down where the octopuses sleep.

I love you huge, I love you vast,
For the fun to come and the fun that's passed.

I love you big, I love you tough,
When the path is smooth and when it's rough.

I love you strong, I love you small,
Together we have it all.

I love you wild, I love you loud,
I shout it out and I feel proud.

I love you soft, I love you still,

And you know I always will . . .

I love you close, I love you tight,

When you're wrong . . . and when you're right.

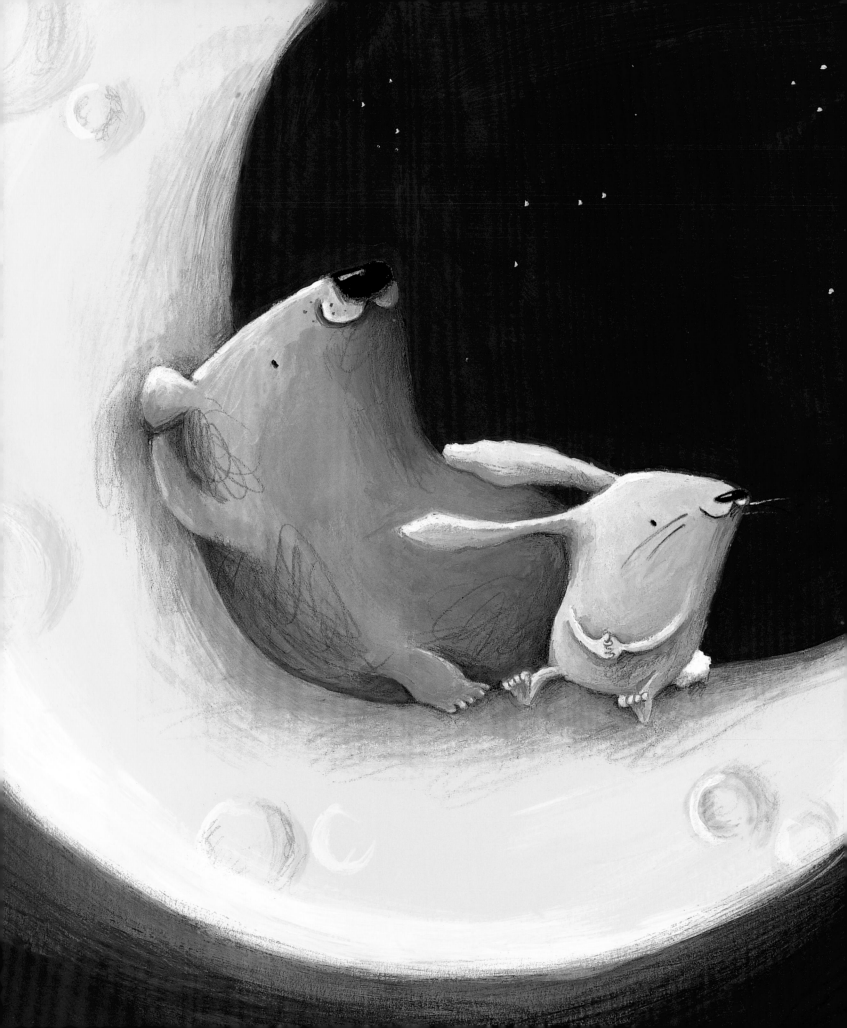

I love you night, I love you day,
In every moment, come what may . . .

Because I love you with my whole heart,

From where you end . . . to where you start.

For Mum—Aama, we love you most, we love you best,
we love you to bits . . . to crumbs . . . to cinnamon tea
~S. P.-H. & the boys

To my mum and dad
~A. B.

First published in Great Britain in January 2014 by Bloomsbury Publishing Plc
Published in the United States of America in June 2014 by Bloomsbury Children's Books
www.bloomsbury.com
Bloomsbury is a registered trademark of Bloomsbury Publishing Plc

For information about permission to reproduce selections from this book, write to
Permissions, Bloomsbury Children's Books, 1385 Broadway, New York, New York 10018
Bloomsbury books may be purchased for business or promotional use. For information on bulk purchases please contact
Macmillan Corporate and Premium Sales Department at specialmarkets@macmillan.com

Text inspired by Ephesians 3:17–19

Library of Congress Cataloging-in-Publication Data
Prasadam, Smriti.
I love you night and day / by Smriti Prasadam-Halls ; illustrated by Alison Brown.
pages   cm
Summary: A sweet message of unconditional love follows a bear and a bunny through their day.
ISBN 978-1-61963-222-6 (hardcover) • ISBN 978-1-61963-223-3 (reinforced)
ISBN 978-1-61963-336-0 (e-book) • ISBN 978-1-61963-391-9 (e-PDF)
[1. Love—Fiction. 2. Bears—Fiction. 3. Rabbits—Fiction.] I. Title.
PZ8.3.P77 Ial 2014   [E]—dc23   2013039383

Typeset in Horley Old Style
Printed in China by C&C Offset Printing Co., Ltd., Shenzhen, Guangdong
4 6 8 10 9 7 5   (hardcover)
2 4 6 8 10 9 7 5 3 1 (reinforced)

All papers used by Bloomsbury Publishing, Inc., are natural, recyclable products made from wood grown in well-managed forests.
The manufacturing processes conform to the environmental regulations of the country of origin.